The Night Before Easter

Grosset & Dunlap

To my mother, who always made
Easter special—N.W.

For my Aunt Vera and Uncle Bozo—
Happy snacking! I love you—K.C.

Grosset & Dunlap, Publishers

Text copyright © 1999 by Natasha Wing. Illustrations copyright © 1999 by Kathy Couri. All rights reserved. Published by Grosset & Dunlap, a division of Penguin Young Readers Group, 345 Hudson Street, New York, New York 10014. GROSSET & DUNLAP is a trademark of Penguin Group (USA) Inc. Published simultaneously in Canada. Printed in the U.S.A.

Library of Congress Cataloging-in-Publication Data
Wing, Natasha.
    The night before Easter / by Natasha Wing ; illustrated by Kathy Couri.
        p. cm. — (Reading railroad books)
    Summary: In this version of Clement Moore's classic poem, two siblings witness the nighttime arrival of the Easter Bunny.
    1. Easter—Juvenile poetry. 2. Rabbits—Juvenile poetry. 3. Children's poetry, American. [1. Easter—Poetry. 2. Rabbits Poetry. 3. Narrative poetry. 4. American poetry.] I. Couri, Kathryn A., ill. II. Title. III. Series: Grosset & Dunlap reading railroad book.
    PS3573.I53145N54   1999
    811'.54—dc21   98-41054
                                                                                                    CIP
                                                                                                    AC

ISBN 978-0-448-41873-5

The Night Before Easter

By Natasha Wing Illustrated by Kathy Couri

'Twas the night before Easter,
just before dawn;
not a creature was stirring
out on the lawn.

Our baskets were set
on the table with care,
in hopes that the Easter Bunny
soon would be there.

Sister and I
were tucked snug in our beds,
while visions of jellybeans
danced in our heads.

Then out in the barn
the hens made such a clatter,
I sprang from my bed
to see what was the matter.

When what to my curious eyes
should appear,
but a big fuzzy rabbit
with a crook in his ear.

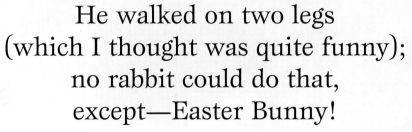

He walked on two legs
(which I thought was quite funny);
no rabbit could do that,
except—Easter Bunny!

He sniffed at a pansy,
a tulip, a rose,

jumped over a shovel,

a rake,

and a hose.

Then up to our house,
in just a few hops,
he came bearing chocolates
and striped lollipops.

As I sat on the stairs
not making a sound,
that swift, dapper Bunny
sprang in with a bound.

His soft fur was spotless
from his head to his toe;
his vest was all checkered;
his tie in a bow.

His eyes—how they sparkled!
His whiskers—how merry!
His tail was like cotton;
his nose like a berry!

He made not a sound,
but went straight to his treasure,
filled up our baskets,
adding more for good measure.

Chocolates and chicks
and candy galore
spilled from our baskets
and onto the floor!

And just when I thought
that the Bunny was done,
he picked out some eggs,
looking over each one.

He carefully hid them
on couches and chairs,
the mantel, the bookshelf,
and under the stairs.

When our rooster crowed,
he turned with a start,
he wiggled his nose,
then went to his cart.

He sprang from the house
with a single bound,
and bounced down the street
without making a sound.

I read his note
as he hop-hopped away:
"Happy Easter to all—
and to all a great day!"